Murder Your Darlings

A Duluth Failed Poets Society Anthology

Book design by Emma L. Verstraete
Cover art by Campbell David

ISBN: 979-8-218-62373-9

Find us on Instagram: @duluthfailedpoetssociety

Content Advisory:

Writing is a vulnerable medium that is used to address challenging themes and topics. Several pieces within this book contain or allude to subject matter that could be upsetting. Just as we wish to share the creations that address grief and painful experiences, we wish to give our readers the chance to prioritize their mental health and well-being. We've made our best effort to include all of the topics that could cause distress.

These sensitive subjects are included on the pages specified:

Body Image: 10, 52, 53
Drug Abuse: 36-37
Fantasy Violence: 34-35
Grief/ Loss: 36-37, 48-49
Miscarriage: 48-49
Self-Harm: 32, 33

Table of Contents

Illustration Credits

Foreword

To the person who purchased this book:

Thank you for supporting the Duluth Failed Poets Society! First of all, we have no affiliation with any Taylor Swift album or Robin Williams movie.

In fact, we are a group of creatives in the Duluth area who come together to challenge and support each other. We are a five-table, vibes-based organization that meets every Monday from 6pm-8pm at the Loch Café & Games. Our vision is to be a safe and productive space for creatives to improve their craft. Our purpose is to develop our skills and grow as artists through honest feedback and discussion.

The intention of this work is to establish a connection with the community in Duluth. Consider this a formal introduction to a group of talented and passionate individuals, intent on expressing our voices to the best of our ability. We also like to show off.

So if you feel like a poet or you feel like a failure, feel free to stop by and join us.

Thank you once again for your contribution to the Duluth Failed Poets Society. There is no higher calling than to be a patron of the arts, supporting the efforts of creative expression in your local community.

To the person who stole this book:

We will see you Monday.

- Alexander Buelt

Trust the Process
Alexander Buelt

I need to meet me eye to eye.
I thought I'd throw a line to find my other side—
the I that lies and hides inside my poetry and fiction,
though he seemingly provides the guides
to diction and description—
a light that shines behind my eyes
when writing is divine inscription.

A direct line to the source of inspiration—
a state of elevation best described as pure elation
dipped in drive, determination and
a little disassociation.

If I could find the guy behind my eyes I might inquire why
the lies I spill are still so tied up in addiction.
The times that he and I decide
to put aside the differences
within our lines of sight lead to
epiphanies and inferences—
a depth, a field of vision I uncover on revision.

Decisions made on instinct in the moment of discovery—
revealing how my body's feeling,
how it needs recovery.
It needs rejuvenation and some healing and some silence—
solitude and rest from all the self defeating violence.

With each interpretation I inspect the current iteration,
holding conversation with
my own imagination.
I grapple with stagnation and unhappiness with my creations—
patience and compassion for my self are not considerations.

No wonder why I always try to undercut that I—
why I keep him shut away from all the people in my life.
Maybe I'm afraid to let him see the light of day
because I worry that the writer and the addict are the same—
the light behind my eyes might be addiction by another name.

I think it's how he comes out when I drink and sleep around
and keep repeating all the dumb mistakes like cheating—
but somehow I've got to tame him,
make him listen to me now.
I glare into the spaces where his eyes should be
and after staring at him long enough I start to see.

I'm wrong about the guy behind my eyes.
He's more than just the parts inside my heart I try to hide.
He exists within my rhymes and repetition in the midst of lines
so I can shine a light into the corners of my mind—
he's the devil on my shoulder and the angel on the other side.

Sure he lacks direction and he often needs correction—
the way he acts is tactless
but the fact is he attracts the
type of magic that allows me to express my inner needs.
Even when they're dressed in indiscretions
I can listen to the lessons that he tries to teach.

Before I go ignoring
the only form of speech he knows,
perhaps I could explore the core of why
he seeks to breach the confines I've imposed.
If I let him say his piece
the two of us might start to see
some peace between the parts of me.

Imperfect Bounty

JE

I am not long and lithe
I am plump
Like fruit on the vine
Heavy with sweetness that many have wished to taste
And I have fed them

My skin is not smooth nor clear nor creamy
The sun has kissed me
The universe has touched me
And left its marks

My hair does not flow nor shine like the sun
It twists and tangles and ensnares
Like roots underground
I like it that way

Shooting stars have left their silver tails in my hair
Maybe remnants of all the wishes I've made

I am not an ethereal being
I am of the earth
Of the Goddess
Of the lakes and rivers that surround me

The lake calls my name and keeps me close
While the river washes away my heartache

My hands are filthy with dirt from gardens I have grown
I have watched them flourish
And left them to decay

I am not long and lithe
I am not clean and clear
I am not ethereal

I am of the earth and its imperfect bounty
And there is beauty in me

Earthworms Have Five Hearts (for Ted Jarosh)

Evan Tungate

I walked home after rain and the air stank
of life and worms swam on the sidewalk and
I thought how good it felt to be alive—
And I thought of you. I walked home under
the sun's loving gaze and those same worms lay
crisp and flat as eggs burnt on the pan and
I thought how good it felt to be alive—
And I thought of you. In your proud garden
in the house where you used to live I'd watch
hummingbirds sip from shaded columbines
and think how good it felt to be alive—
And when I see them now I think of you.
I drove past that house today. Your garden
is gone. Will the hummingbirds understand?

Spider
Rune Peddle

I keep spiders
in my room
because they are my friends.

They are little artists,
just like me.

They whisper
sweet nothings
and stories of shadows.

They remind me that
I am
The Life Weaver,
that I craft this existence.

They show me that I should
tread lightly,
like a dancer,
and to suck the magic
out of every opportune
moment.

They whisper
in my ear at night
"No thread is meaningless
in the tapestry of life."

The Monkey Poem
Scott Neby

Two monkeys sit in a clearing
and gaze upon the stars
They pick fleas from each other's coats
and wonder at it all

But wonder turns to worry
as life's scale becomes more clear
One monkey turns to the other
and gives voice to their fear

"When Monkey climb a tree
Monkey feel big and tall
but when Monkey look at twinkly lights
Monkey feel so small
little like a flea
like Monkey's life of climbing tree
does not matter at all!"

The second monkey chimes in
a new fear in their eye
as they explain the truth
of what said statement must imply

"If Monkey like a flea
then fur is like a tree
then there must be Big Space Monkey
who will groom out you and me!"

(The monkeys didn't know how far to push analogy.)

The first monkey responded
that they knew what to do
"Maybe if Monkey offers gifts to sky
then Monkey won't be groomed!"

So the monkeys gathered rocks and sticks
and bugs and fruit and leaves
Anything of value
so that they might appease
the Monkey in the Sky enough
that it might leave them be

But the second monkey worried
that this wouldn't be enough
"What if Space Monkey doesn't care
about ground monkey stuff?
Maybe to appease it
we need to show it love!"

So the monkeys shouted praises
to some distant point in space
but they knew two feeble voices
could never reach that place

The monkeys knew what they needed
They had to gather up the troop
What they couldn't do alone
they could accomplish as a group

So the two monkeys set out
to spread their knowledge far and wide
so that every monkey knew
about the Monkey in the Sky

And when they all gathered together
to shout praises into space
our two monkeys were leaders
of an entire monkey faith

And then the faith expanded
in the way religions do
so there was a set of knowledge
that every monkey knew

Like how Space Monkey liked bananas
but didn't like them green
or how praises must be shouted
in a hearty monkey scream

Or how Space Monkey holds the world
in a mighty monkey hug
but if a monkey's bad
they'll be groomed out like a bug

Or how the two monkey founders
must have the biggest tallest tree
so that they may be closer
to the Mighty Space Monkey

And on that tree two monkeys sit
in gentle reverie
"Tell me friend what was it
that so troubled you and me?"

"Monkey was so worried
that twinkly light make him small
but now we know Space Monkey
is the best monkey of all!"

"Look what Space Monkey gave us
We're in the biggest tree
Plus all the offered fruits
actually go to you and me."

"Monkey barely remembers
what our worries were about
Some kind of silly existential dread
So glad we figured that one out."

Faded
Justin Rose

Green wings glow in the grey
of dawn's early, dull dimness.
Another would say, see the Luna soar,
but I see the Fairy that fades in the morn'.
The silent swift Fairy who, only half-real,
flits through the forests of Vermont's green hills.
So few are left who see them, fewer who can find
the last remaining hideaways, where these marvels lie.
But I still sigh at the sight of their lights
as they wing 'midst the fireflies at night
and stir idle, rippling rings round the raindrop's plop.
The wise, the blind, they shake grave heads
and scoff with voices cold.
They tell me as they stumble, long white canes outstretched,
To see the world for what it is. But if the world
must gray my soul, if it must dull my sight,
then I would find the Fairies' forest
and leave man to his angles and lines.
I hear them whisper in the wind.
I strain to sift their songs and see
the meaning of their melodies.
But so faint are the Fairies now,
so lost to the world, that they
barely show themselves or speak
before their lights decay.
Oh, weep for the fairies, wild
children, you who see them still.
For soon they shall fade forever
and depart from Vermont's green hills.

The Day the Soldiers Came
Aubrey Day

My back was bent and hooves sunk deep in the zhavo field when the soldiers came. My son stared at them, open-mouthed, with an expression working towards furious until I elbowed him roughly. He put his head down, keeping one square pupil focused sideways on them.

"That's not our uniform, what are soldiers from another City doing here?!"

I shook my head; an ache that had begun from the sun gleaming off the water was building behind my eyes. I reached to wipe the sweat from my brow and only managed to smear mud across the roots of my horns. Sam's impatient gaze hounded me as I leaned on my hoe.

"Would you like to go ask them?" My forced jovial tone didn't amuse, judging by the glare he leveled at me. "Bah, we will know when they need us to know." I hoped to dispel his interest; my son held to things in frightening ways sometimes. He had argued into the curled horns of the most bull-headed taurun merchants, and even with guards in the city when he felt they were unfairly treating us. I grasped for something that could justify their presence. "Maybe they mean to call up soldiers for a counter-attack against the barbarians."

He seemed to take that answer and we went back to weeding the field. I was disquieted, though, and unable to fall peacefully back into our task. I had seen soldiers from Greystone, the only City with authority to make attacks, and what I saw now was not the uniform of Greystone Keep.

The line of soldiers marched with a sort of casual order that I found worrying, chatting with each other and looking out over the fields. They were armored, not in casual clothes or parade gear: the bird brothers in scout armor that left their flight mobility uncompromised and the wolf brothers in heavier armor which, to my eye, looked miserable to march in. We goats of the field kept our heads down as we worked; I felt we had a group instinct to stay below their notice. The end of the row showed more discipline than the front and I saw why: a pair of officers led from the rear.

The first of the riders was a wolf brother whose golden-yellow eyes scanned the landscape with a gaze sharp enough to pierce. He was the one who led these soldiers, judging by the marshal's star on his uniform, though his blood was visibly thinner than I would have expected for such a position, his flat simply-bearded face odd for a luphir.

The other, oddly, was not his bird brother but a nobleman who, in opposition to the marshal, had nearly the full face of a panther, his high gold-bedecked ears and black velvet fur showing him to be of pristine lineage. My unease grew. For what purpose had they sent these soldiers with some soft-pawed consort in place of a politician? He looked over the zhavo as they rode and I felt exposed, as though he took special care to look at each of us in turn.

The weight of the soldier's passing held us down long after they had passed. We strained our ears through the afternoon for noise of action but it never came and finally; as the sun approached the evening mountains we dragged ourselves home. Or maybe that was just me, maybe I was the only old goat still working the fields, back permanently bent, mud stuck in my hooves weighing them down, dragging myself home in the evening. I sighed and leaned on my hoe, stopping for a moment. Sam looked at me with concern.

"All right, father?"

I scoffed. "Boy, can't a man take a moment to breathe in Uoni's light?"

He was quiet a long moment. "Father, do you really think *those* soldiers are here to recruit *our* soldiers?"

It was my turn for a long pause. I had to give him a way to understand, to make sense of them. Sam had an *intensity* to him when he didn't understand something and I knew he would take no thought for his own safety to find his answers. I couldn't lie to him though; I had learned as he became an adult that, as simple as he seemed in regards to other's reaction to him, he was no fool. Honesty was my only tool and gave him the best answer I had.

"I... do not. I didn't recognize their uniform; they weren't from any City with any nice reason to be here. I don't know what they mean to do but they have no quarrel with us. We are capria, we are beneath the soldiers, so far that we are beneath their notice entirely. Whatever they do in the city they still need the zhavo."

This at last seemed to satisfy him and we made our way home.

***

When I woke, the house felt cold and lonely. I shuffled out of my pallet as soon as I could manage and knew immediately what was wrong. Sam's pallet was not just empty but rolled and stored. He had written a message on the counter top.

"Gone to town,
be back, don't worry.
Sorry,
Sam"

My veins ran with ice and the charcoal letters swam in my vision. I had failed him. He'd gone to search out the truth for himself. I grabbed a rag and scrubbed the counter clean in a hysterical fit of energy. I had to find him.

It was wrong of me to abandon the field but I wouldn't make much headway on my own anyway so, with heavy heart and hooves, I took up my walking stick and headed into the City.

The fit stone of the road pushed on my spine in ways the soft mud of the *zhavo* fields never did. I wasn't made to walk a road like this.

The morning sun was high before I made it to the wooden gates. The Bird and Wolf at the gate were unfamiliar to me, in the uniform of the encroaching army, but they didn't bar me from entering.

A crier was calling people together in the square. Murmurs moved through the assembling crowd but quietly, too quiet for such a large group. I got closer, slowly, painfully, clutching my stick with now-shaking arms. The crier stood on the wooden stand that served all purposes that bring people together: festivals, speeches, or executions. Our marshal stood on the stage with him, her beautiful feathers tucked slim to her body in a fear that didn't show on her face. The luphir who led the interlopers stood behind her with three pairs of Brothers at attention. They watched the crowd with a predatory hunger, as though daring us to challenge them and discover the consequences.

Finally the marshal raised her arms and what little noise had inhabited the crowd died with a whimper.

"Friends, neighbors, people of Greenfield! By now we have all heard the murmuring of a crisis in the capital. We have discouraged the spreading of baseless rumors, but now I bring you the true story. I will not treat you like children with pretty language; the situation is indeed dire. The Heir has been assassinated and the Queen in the holy depth of her grief has abdicated her throne."

Her words washed through the crowd like the rains flooding the fields.

"Assassinated?"

—but the Queen?"

"—abdicated?"

The rasping whispers and rising panic of the assembled set my horns itching with the tension to flee, but she silenced us again.

"This is Marshal Bardon."

The thin-blooded luphir stepped forward to sternly survey the crowd. The nobleman who had ridden in with him was nowhere to be seen.

"He and his soldiers are here at the generous mercy of the Matriarch of Highgarden to bastion and safeguard our fair valley. They are here to protect the fields and ensure the production of zhavo is not disturbed by this time of unrest. Please respect them as you would any soldier of Greenfield. Any threat to our security in this unsettled time must be taken extremely seriously. Any citizen that refuses to respect the authority of this peace will be considered to have publicly renounced it and will be treated as such. Go about your lives as normal. We are the children of Firendz, we have always lived in His peace, and we shall keep it!" She put her arms down and the crowd slowly drifted away like the morning mist.

I scanned the crowd with weary desperation. Sam should be here, he *must* be here, there was nowhere else he needed to be to learn about the soldiers…. He wasn't here. My heart fell so fast my head spun and I sat hard on the side of the road. My soul pushed at me, begging me to stand and search for him, to comb the streets in fruitless pursuit, but my weary legs refused. Hope soured in my soul and my eyes burned. I knew I wouldn't find him.

***

It was days later when I heard they had put up a gallows in the square. The pain of his absence had already dulled; his mother's death had primed me for it years ago. I didn't need the careful, oh-so-gentle, faces of the ones who came from the city to work the fields to tell me that my son was one of the wretches who swung.

Pay Back the Sun
Nannette Montgomery

You're right, friend,
I should pay back the sun
for this raspberry sweet on my tongue
brings back young days
when picking berries for one blistering summer.
Old lady Johnson would lean across
the table during my lunch break,
her only employee,
she pounded sense into me
about lying politicians
and the greedy IRS.
Don't ever trust a political man
or his wife,
and don't ever pay one cent
more to the government
than you have to.
The bums get enough already.
She'd slap her coffee cup down
for exclamation
then tell me to get back to the berries.
I'm not paying you to sit here and listen to me
talk bullshit, girl.
Damn. I love raspberries.

Nostalgia
Kristina Braaten-Lee

When you are a woman of *un certain âge* everything—or nearly everything—brings on the affliction of nostalgia. A song, for example. Or a movie that you've watched already at least three times. A photograph. An old letter or occasional card tucked in a favorite book you just took out of storage.

Just the other day, I opened an old paperback given me by my French sister, *Le Soulier de Satin* by Paul Claudel. It was underlined throughout, and short comments were written in the margins in French. She must have sent it to me in the United States.

Tucked in the middle of the book was a tiny card with these perfectly penned words:

> *Joyeux Noël ma chère soeur,*
> *à toi et à ta famille*
> *Bonne Année!*
> *Ta soeur, Christine*

The longer comments were written in 1977. Did I ever get back to her? Lydia wondered. Did I ever read the book? If I do now, will I live with regret for the rest of my life? Or, will it just be another reminder of how many years are gone and how much is forgotten? So that's what I'm thinking of now when I hear or read the word *nostalgia*. But here's a live memory! Just happened to bring it to mind. Nostalgia it is!

Armand and I were trying to find an exceptional restaurant that my parents and we could enjoy. In other words—not Culver's. Not Perkins. Not The Ranch House that smelled of slightly curdled ranch dressing and congealed bacon grease. What we landed on was an Indian restaurant called Kurry Kebab. I had to fast-talk my folks into agreeing to dine there. Shrimp and rice in curry sauce made with coconut milk was the menu item that persuaded them, but not without a conference on sodium.

My father in his later years worried about his blood pressure. So the waitress brought the chef to our table to compare sodium levels in lamb, seafood, and vegetarian dishes. After my father's apology to the chef for getting old—"though having originated in a country where elders are revered"—my mother got this puckish expression on her face. In a tone I'd almost call flirtatious, she said, "And having come from a place where everyone wants to be young forever, I'm telling you that I could outrun you, hands down!" The chef's eyes widened, the waitress and I broke into loud laughter, and a basket of naan appeared warm and aromatic with garlic and cilantro.

And the shrimp? Those synchronized swimmers in a pool of pink coconut cream curry seduced us into silence. No more talk of sodium or a world gone mad. We ate and ate, all appetite now, and dreamed of evenings past when the sun sank slowly into the Indian Ocean and my father sang *Abide with me, fast falls the eventide* in his deep voice. And Mom and Dad and all of us were young.

Visiting in Quiet Evening Hours...

Dana W. Maijala

Porchlight filters amid red pines
Threshold from one quiet home to another
Piecing a path through snow and ice

When there was a tilted, tired shed on the corner
When there was a nestling batch of bushes 'round it
Our footpaths found the hill's steeper incline

Today, I step slowly along the gentler route
Their driveway bearing all traveling weight
Wondering just what year the unruly bushes
    were tamed, and the shed retired

Winding hours blend our long shadows
Twilight wistful of youthful anecdotes,
    now traded for muted observations

Having leisurely grown perspective high above
Red pines sway, reaching their full height
Do the trees see the differences in us?

Quiet pines overhead
Quiet folks within

The Last Book on Earth
Corey Roysdon

It's been a long time since I've been to the beach.

Well, do you count the lakeshore? I don't. I mean a *real* beach.

I mean fine sand too hot for your feet. I mean kids shouting in mock terror at the waves coming up to their necks. I mean feeling the salt hit your lungs like a menthol cigarette, sharp and soothing in a slightly masochistic kind of way. Reggae music blasting from a shitty boombox on the boardwalk while barefoot skaters on bamboo pintails weave their way through the mass collection of tourists who don't know where they're going and locals who don't care where they're going.

You just can't get that at a lake.

I wish this beach was like what I remember.

I guess the changes happened here the same time they happened everywhere else, but I don't really know exactly when they happened everywhere else either. Everything I had known about The End when I was younger was that it happened all at once, when we least expected it. Life would go on until it didn't, no warning. Like a thief in the night. That didn't end up being the case, but hey, hindsight's 20/20.

No, things started to change long before I arrived, and I suppose they will continue to do so until they reach some sort of stasis. After all, that's what happens when people leave. They take everything with them, their belongings, their essentials, their families. Their stories. When nobody else is left, nothing that was left behind is of any value. It's just that, a memory. Forgotten.

That's why this book is so important.

After The End, I walked for months just to get back home. I wanted to see it. I wanted to see what it was, not what it is now.

Life is full of disappointments.

The sand is littered with the remains of my old coastal town. The ocean tried to take most of it back, but I guess it didn't like the taste, because it continued to spit it all back out onto the shore. Broken pieces of wave-tumbled glass and driftwood, plastic bags and soda bottles stolen from a boardwalk store, seaweed and volleyball nets tangled together, locking sea creatures in a foul smelling prison.

What I wouldn't give to see it all how it once was in real time.

I'll take what I can get.

I used to always get so angry walking into a bookstore and seeing a book wrapped in plastic; what's the point? Aren't books for reading? I chalked it all up to corporate greed, big businesses wanting us to pay top dollar and willing to protect their profits at all costs. But now, oh man. If they could see their work now.

Walking down this discarded city I used to call a home, amidst all the garbage and death and destruction, sticking half-buried out of the sand is one stunning pop of color.

A book cataloging what this town used to be.

Photos of the past, neatly wrapped in a protective plastic coating.

The last book on earth.

A story of what home used to be.

Transitions
Bug

I.
I worship the orb weaver in the backyard
      so diligently constructing her web.
She will destroy it come morning
      only to build it once again.
I admire her dedication.
One must imagine the spider forgetful
      focused solely on the web of today.
Before I can ask,
      she is gone.
And I mourn the piece of sky she framed.

II.
I witness the monarch caterpillars
      as I play god on my balcony.
It's a numbers game.
The monarch butterfly will lay four hundred eggs;
      only eight of them will reach adulthood.
Despite my clumsy hands,
      I shepherd along about that many.
I marvel at their single-mindedness.
No time to question as they dissolve into something new
      just a magnetic trust in the process.
And as I leave them behind for my next journey,
      I wish the same for me.

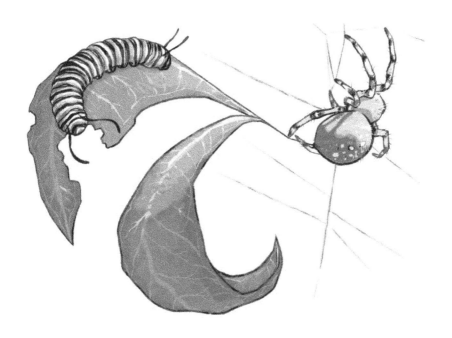

Little Bird
Justin Rose

The little singer sprightly springs,
gently flutt'ring fragile wings.
He stabs the slender stalks of plants
then shakes them till they dance.

The trembling leaves trickle light
in dappled droplets, scattered bright,
that spatter cross his speckled down,
to run and drip upon the ground.

But frail fellow, small and slight,
the plant remains quite whole despite
your wild assaults.

The little writer, like the bird,
wildly lashes out in word,
raging at life's mighty trunk,
striking, fuming, helpless, drunk.

But only weak, scattered beams
of life pass the shaken leaves.
No revelation, vast insight,
can he shake down with all his might.

See, little writer, small and slight,
life moves on and on despite
your wild assaults.

When you fade,
life still lives, not a leaf unmade.

Swallowed Words

Emma L. Verstraete

Yesterday I choked on my words.

I choked on my words and swallowed my pride and
       admitted I missed you.
I bit back my confessions and adulations and
       smothered the bile back down.
I took my opinions and ideas and gulped them down
       like forgotten wine.
I swallowed my words and left them to burn in my stomach acid
       and regrets.
I suffocated under the weight of our contradictions
       and let the things left unsaid stifle me.

Today I put you away and screamed my ideas
       and promised to leave nothing unsaid ever again.

Tomorrow I'll give voice to my demons
       their words were never yours to take.

hell's kitchen poetry

Anastasia Bamford

the pressure is on
words slashing
across the blank page

i am carving
pieces of myself
plating it for
consumption
and judgement

is it burning?
yeah, but that's
what i wanted
too complex or
not enough going on?

screw it
if you worry
about the judges
you'll never
write anything

when you cut
yourself
keep going

Draining
Alyssa Stellar

There must be something there that mimics the fall of the helicopter leaf. I'd meet someone: my father maybe, or his. They would say loving things to me. They would tell stories of my childhood, and share the thoughts I had never told before. Their words would flow sweetly like honey down my throat, sticking to my tongue so I might finally have something nice to say. My mouth would open, and the world would rush in. The water trickling down my lungs would burn like the fire that illuminated our laughs the last time we were together in our worn camp chairs. Surely, a stifled breath would be as peaceful as my grandmother's voice or the music by the bay, welcoming me home to their soft tune. I believe there will be beauty there. I'll see lights as bright as the stars Orion wears, feel the gentle scratch of grass from the gardens we played in as children, run my hands through your hair, and breathe. I wonder; will you be disappointed? You have always said there are many joys life can afford. Though I have never felt joy from afforded goods, other than the cracked mirror and glass bowl in my kitchen, I have found joy in the living. The isopods squirming through the root-bound forest of my terrariums know the greatest truths of life—the fungus, mold, and decay that come with its end. I hope they will meet me there too. I suppose, however, if I were to die they would have no one left. Maybe my purpose here is to experience the joy in living, not being. There is something. The crumpled napkins at the bar on First Avenue, streaked by the mess of splitting melted mozzarella over a table too long to manage, must mean more than we give them credit for. It is in the air on the pier, where the sea spray stains the glass I collect to remind myself that my world is worth more than the bottom of the ocean. Companionship, creation. Maybe these are experiences only life can afford.

Oh, look. My tub has overflowed.

Two Years on a Mermaid Farm
Evan Tungate

After I graduated with my associate's in Fishery Sciences I did two years as a tech on a mermaid farm in Norway. It was unsettling, at first. I'd be working on the big floating pens and look down into the water and see, alongside the scales flashing as they caught the light, a perfect naked torso like a Playboy spread. Just for a second, and then it would be gone. The old salts gave me a hard time whenever they caught me staring. You'll get over it, they laughed. They were right.

A few months in I moved on to a different crew, working as a feeder for two-fifty more an hour. We'd scoop protein-fortified cornmeal from fifty-gallon drums and the water would boil and they'd rise like piranhas. Their hair was a perfect glossy black and their eyes were dark and completely empty. They liked it the most when we'd toss in kitchen scraps. Vegetable peels and rinds. Gristle and bone and fat skimmed off the top. They'd sing for that, low keening tones that always set my teeth on edge. I started sleeping with earplugs in. They denied me workers' comp for my tinnitus.

It takes three to four years for a mermaid to reach their adult weight and at that point they're ready for harvest. I hear there's a new breed some of the farms down in Tasmania and New Zealand are raising now that takes half that, but the industry was just getting started back then. The farm I worked on had eight pens in their rotation, so every six months the whole place would get assigned to processing. It was hard, exhausting work. I've never slept so good. We'd draw in the nets around each pen until the mermaids were packed tight and thrashing, then we'd snag 'em around the neck with catch poles and drag 'em onto the deck. I got pretty good at that. They'd be singing the whole time, of course, just this awful banshee wailing. A couple of the guys would get nosebleeds but I never did.

Once they were on the deck it'd take two or three men, and it was always men, no women ever worked on the farm when I was there, to hold the mermaid down. Each one was four or five feet long, but the tail was solid muscle so they'd weigh about two hundred, maybe a little more. At first they gave us the same tools for salmon, these Japanese things, ikejime, that we were supposed to drive right into the mermaid's hindbrain for a humane kill. It didn't work most of the time, since they have thick skulls and small brains and a lot of empty space in their heads for acoustics or buoyancy or whatever, so guys would just swing and swing and swing until the flopping stopped. Messy work, especially before they started giving us face shields. Some of the real old-timers could slip it right in and pulp the brainstem, like a biologist pithing a frog, and I always tried to wind up on their harvesting crews when I could. A year in, they switched us over to captive bolt pistols and that made things a lot easier. Just a quick pop and their pupils would blow and the tail would twitch once, maybe, and the fingers would curl up and that was that.

I never worked in processing so I can't speak to that so much. The tails went on ice right away, I know, but the upper bodies just went overboard. I'm not a mermaid biologist so I couldn't tell you if they were inedible or just not profitable. Not a lot of meat on those bones. So they'd get dumped over the side with the rest of the offal and I can tell you about that, all right. Just a rusty smear across the ocean as we made our slow way south and the seabirds came down to pick out those dark eyes before the sharks dragged 'em under.

They sell frozen mermaid filets at Costco now. They're a little lighter and flakier than salmon, with a slight taste of fennel. Definitely give them a try.

Charybdis
Alexander Buelt

How long since you slept?
Down in the depths of a stimulant binge
Haunted by ghosts of dirty syringes
There's no doubt you're strung out and most of it hinges
On whether it's better to love and to lose
And weather the storm as it gathers and brews
Or to stay down and lie in the dirt

I know that it hurts in your heart and your head
And part of you died in that hospital bed
But the rain's coming down now
I can't watch you drown now or get washed away
In a flood of tears and poisoned blood
The earth is melting into mud
There's nothing I could ever say
To fix the hand that fate has dealt you
Nothing I can do to help you take away the fear and pain
'Cause I can't stop the rain from falling
I can only stand here calling you to get back up again
Begging you to let me be your friend

The ending depends upon how you respond
I've seen what will happen and trust me it's wrong
To sit here while the water rises, slowly losing hope
Compromising everything to helplessness and dope
The waves are crashing all around us
We don't have a rope
This time when the riptide takes us
We won't have a boat to save us
No one's here to tow us back to shore

I can't do this anymore
I won't succumb to what will come
If I don't turn and run for dry land
Please understand, this isn't me stranding you
I swear I'll come back and reach out my hand
Once I know what it is I should do
It's hard to be sober and you'll never be over her
But one corpse is better than two

Of course you're gone by the time I return
By then we're picking out an urn
And singing Monty Python hymns about the brighter side
Reading all your journal entries
Seeing just how hard you tried
To stay afloat and fight the tide
Our mothers say you made some strides
In the months before the day you died
But what burns me up and churns my insides
Is that just before the lights went dim
They saw you learning how to swim

Love Poem for a Double Agent
Evan Tungate

When we kiss your tongue dances
on my suicide tooth.
My favorite kind of wet work.
I want to meet you in Saint James's Park to feed the ducks
and each other
breadcrumbs.

Wrap me in your arms razor-wire
and keep me out of the floodlights
as we cross the border again and again and again.
When your controller asks
deny me.

I'm not your Winter Soldier but
you can be my handler. See what trips my wire.
Whisper number-station nothings in my ear.
Beg me to come in
from the cold.

Jim

Corey Roysdon

Jim is a normal guy.

However you think a normal guy looks, that's pretty much it. You can't put in too much thought when it comes to Jim. He wears normal clothes and says normal things. Jim rides his bike to work, to stay active and in shape. Jim likes to cook, and tolerates washing dishes. Jim listens to podcasts while he cleans and while he works on his hobbies. Jim builds model airplanes in his free time.

Jim has lived in the same town his whole life. He's lived in three different apartments, but they've all been on the edge of downtown. Jim shops at the same grocery store every week, and he buys normal things like fruit and bread and cheese and butter and mayonnaise. He gets coffee at the same coffee shop every morning. Jim is a normal guy.

Jim has a pet cat. It's a normal cat, a fat tabby that sleeps most of the time. He sleeps on the edge of the bed with Jim. The cat's name is a normal cat's name, because it is a normal cat. Sometimes, when Jim is at work, the cat will follow him out and watch him work. Sometimes the cat will hunt for birds and lizards. The cat will always be home before Jim comes home. Jim doesn't know that his cat leaves every day. Jim might be angry if he did know. Not too angry; Jim loves his cat the normal amount.

Jim doesn't understand his job. Jim doesn't know why he does what he does.

Jim has a normal job, stacking boxes in the woods. He locks his bike up at the trailhead and walks into the forest, under the canopy of trees and the watchful eye of the birds that tell him not to go. He wanders off the beaten path into the creek, and wades his way under the bridges, through brown water and algae-covered rocks, never slipping, never breaking stride. He stops when he finds a pile of cardboard boxes in the water, thrown from directions untraceable, and he removes them from the creek and stacks them up on the rocks. Some of the boxes are cold, half falling apart from the water damage. Some of the boxes are heavier than the others, Jim puts these on the bottom of the stacks. Some boxes have crimson stains, the contents shifting and dripping and softly whimpering. Some boxes are hot, and do not cool down.

      Jim doesn't ask many questions. He doesn't talk much. Jim has wondered why he does this job. But he would never ask. He wouldn't know who to ask. He can pay the bills, and can afford coffee and to go to the movies every now and then. That's enough for Jim. Jim is a normal guy.

The Leopard
Trae Kryzer

The sharp spade bites into the damp earth beneath my knees, slicing through roots and weeds tangled in the muck. The smell of soil clings to the cool air. I scoop another clump of dirt into the bucket Tommy holds, his gloved fingers tapping impatiently against its rim.

"Time to head back inside?" he asks, eyes scanning the gray horizon, hoping for a sign that we could quit.

I look up at our old house, the same place we've called home for two years, where keeping the lights on feels like a miracle we're always one step from losing. My gaze drifts to the bedroom window, where my lava lamp twists and churns in endless blues and greens. Its hypnotic motion unsettles me today, like it knows a secret I don't.

Tommy shifts the bucket to his other hand, grunting as he hauls it toward the white F-150 parked near the treeline. He stacks it neatly alongside three others in the truck bed, aligning each with obsessive precision. Double-checking. Triple-checking they're secure. The sight would almost be funny if I didn't feel like a lava lamp myself, bubbles stretching and collapsing in a rhythmic torment—twisting the insides of my stomach.

When he turns, arms crossed over his chest, his glare hits me square in the gut. "You okay, or are you gonna stand there having a staring contest with the dirt?"

"Sorry." I brush my muddy fingers against my blue jeans.

"Just... thirsty. I'm heading inside."

The words barely carry, muffled by the thick, stagnant air. The tension clings to everything today—like something invisible clawing at my mind, waiting to strike. That gnawing feeling digs deeper with every step I take toward the house, its weight pressing at the back of my skull.

As I round the corner, my eyes drift to the balcony above, drawn by unconscious habit more than intention. The colorful tapestry hanging there sways gently in the breeze, a bright defiant banner against the gloom of overcast skies. Tommy won it at the carnival yesterday, a prize for some game he won with a lucky shot. His girlfriend probably rolling her eyes while he gloated.

I let myself smile faintly, knowing no one else will appreciate it. No one else can; we're tucked too deep in these woods, miles from anything resembling civilization. Isolation wraps around us like a dense fog, thick enough to choke on if you breathe too deeply.

But something shifts behind the tapestry—a flicker of movement, almost imperceptible. My chest tightens before I even know why. My foot shifts backwards, muscles clenching and preparing for battle. A leopard sits there, ready to pounce.

Its body is sleek, powerful—but wrong. The fur isn't dappled like it should be. Black and white stripes carve across its muscular frame, like a zebra from a fever dream. It doesn't belong here. A contradiction that sticks out like a tear in the fabric of reality.

She watches me. Hollow eyes, neither hostile nor curious—just *waiting*. A predator frozen in the moment before chaos ensues.

My body freezes. The world narrows to the space between us, thick with an awful stillness. No breath, no sound, just the brittle edge of anticipation. One wrong move and it all shatters.

I try to step back, but my heel catches Tommy. My pulse spikes as I spin towards him, words clawing at my throat but breaking into nonsense on the way out. "Gh—gah!"

Tommy blinks, brow furrowed, like I tried to explain calculus in a dream. "What?"

My arms flail uselessly, wild gestures at the thing lurking behind us. I need him to see it, to understand—but the fear tangles my thoughts into static.

Tommy's frown deepens. "Dude, you're freaking me out—what's wrong?"

Still, he doesn't look back. He doesn't see. And that makes it worse.

My voice finally stumbles free, desperate and shaky, "There's a leopard!"

Tommy blinks slowly and then laughs. A sharp bark of disbelief. "Are you serious right now?"

He takes a step backwards to give himself some breathing room.

A step towards the leopard.

Shit.

That step—small and thoughtless—is a trigger pulled. A mistake you can't take back. You don't retreat from a predator, not one this wrong, this impossible. You don't turn your back on something that defies the rules of what's real and imaginary.

My heart lurches, every nerve screaming. I glance back at the thing lounging above us. Its body tenses, muscles rippling beneath that warped, stretched skin. Black and white stripes coil like static on an old TV, flickering just wrong enough to gnaw at the edges of sanity.

It's ready to pounce.

Tommy doesn't see it. He's still laughing, oblivious.

Panic seizes me, fast and stupid. My body moves before my thoughts catch up. The shovel's already in the air, spinning wildly from my hand.

Time slows to a halt.

The dull clang of metal against wood echoes like the punchline to some cosmic joke. The balcony rattles under the blow, but the leopard doesn't flinch. Doesn't blink. It crouches lower, hind legs coiling, fully engaged now—ready.

Tommy, utterly detached, bursts into a wheezing fit of laughter. He doubles over, gasping like he's lost his grip on reality altogether.

"Oh my God," I whisper, my voice trembling. He's gone. Lost in hysteria while I'm standing here unraveling, terror-stricken, trying to hold the pieces together.

I look back at the leopard, heart thundering. My breath catches, bracing for claws, for teeth, for the end—

"You like what my girlfriend won at the carnival?" Tommy says.

And then it hits me.

The leopard.

It's not moving.

It's never moved.

Because it's just a stuffed animal.

Reel Love
Kaely Danielson

Cut!
The connection ends there,
the set and the actors go back to their starting places
and the blunders and mistakes are forgotten.
Take two!
We redo the lines, the scene:
the kiss in the rain that makes the viewers' hearts swell
as they swoon and yearn for that
kind of love—a love like in the movies
where the gestures are grand and one size fits any,
where love strikes at first sight
like an arrow through the heart
and the crescendo of the music hits
at just the right moment
when the leading man gets the girl
because he runs through the airport just barely before it's too late,
or shouts up to the third floor window with a boombox in tow
declaring undying affection and admiration
that blossomed from friendship or dislike or that one night stand
that turned out to be so, so much more.
So many people spend a lifetime looking for that
kind of love—but not me.
I want a love that's undeniably real
with mistakes so good they have to be included.
I want uncontrollable laughter
where my face hurts more than my heartstrings
and the best moments are unscripted surprises,
caught on camera only by serendipitous chance.
Please don't love me like they do in the movies,
love me like we're in the blooper reel.

Bury Me in Salt
Emma L. Verstraete

No, darling, I'm serious. Bury me in salt when the time comes. It sounds unnecessary and dramatic, but frankly so am I. It's one of the few times that magic and science completely agree. Salt protects. Be it witches, demons, bacteria, or decomposition—the answer is salt. Somehow Irish cunning folk and ancient Egyptian priests and a scientist somewhere in a Kraft foods lab have all come to the same conclusion and that has to mean something.

Bury me in salt so in 1500 years archaeologists can stare at my tattoos and jewelry while making wild claims of ritual importance. So someone can put a slice of my stomach on a glass slide and declare that Americans in unprecedented times relied on sourdough, peanut butter, and coffee for sustenance. Tell them to look at my Converse with their orthopedic insoles and declare that I favored form and function.

Bury me in salt so that horrible hag from down the lane can't turn me into a zombie. So she can't call to my spirit with the strands of hair I always leave twisted in my wake. Make sure some enterprising witch can't use a newspaper clipping to force my reflection to do her bidding in the shadow realm for all eternity.

Bury me in salt so that I never have to imagine my face swollen and distended from a putrid combination of hydrogen sulfide and methane. So that I don't have visions of maggots crawling out of my eyes and across my chest. Please ensure that my adipose tissue never melts into a perfect halo around my corpse.

Bury me in salt so that demon we summoned as teenagers can't wear my skin to the high school reunion. So that my afterlife isn't plagued with nightmares of cannibalism and screams for mercy. Leave me secure in the knowledge that no one can call my karma due.

Unnamed
Kapriah Latifé

I close my eyes and tip my head back, lifting to welcome the light drizzle on a July day. Droplets cascade down my face and hair, curling the locks into subtle ringlets.

On my front steps I sit, drenched in warm rain and existing in a peaceful haze.

A girl, looking to be about 9 years old, tiptoes onto the step I've been residing on for who knows how long.
The girl sits down and sighs, oddly mature for her age. She looks at me, then up into the sky, and then at my clothes. Her eyebrows raise in question.

I shrug. "I like the rain."

I look out into the distance, not seeing much at all. The world is quiet. I take a deep breath and reminisce on how we got here.

Motion sickness, raised resting heart rate, fatigue, raise in temperature, a skipped period, a skipped heartbeat, and two little pink lines that replaced the gravity keeping me to the earth.

It's funny how fast the world changes when you realize you *are* the world for something so small.
It's funnier how fast something so tiny can alter your entire existence.
It's even funnier yet how fast panic morphs into hope.

A collage of Pinterest boards of ideas on how to tell the people I love most. Little things that could make this even more special. New traditions I couldn't wait to start. Magic I would get to create. A beautiful world to illustrate.

A whole new life, regardless of the one who helped create it, that I vowed to care for on my own. My body as shelter until my wisdom and care could take over.

I wasn't scared.

I was made for this.

I now know the reason they are called "mama bears".

The flood of hormones that gave me the power to kill if something thought to threaten my new little love. I would stand in protection internally and externally. Protection from parts of the world that will never get to her the way they got to me.

Allowing myself to fixate upon the girl, my grandmother's eyes shine back at me. My mother's immaculate cheekbones rising around eyes that crinkle just like mine do. Her moisture-saturated hair flows down into my soft, subtle curls.

No words can express my love for this girl and all of the familiar pieces that came together to make something so unique. Something that was always too good to be true.

My miracle girl, just close enough to admire.
Yet, she will never be close enough to hold.

I open my eyes, the pseudo raindrops dripping down my cheeks. I let them flow as I curl up in the bathtub, watching the water run red.

I close my eyes to catch one final glimpse of her.

"I miss you already," I sniffle.

"That's silly, I'm right here."

She giggles, scoots a little closer to me, leans her head against my shoulder and sighs,

"I like the rain too."

A Religious Guilt
Alyssa Stellar

When I was young,
each home I visited kept
a suitcase full of saints
in the attic
for   safekeeping.

Each occupant:
flesh
        body
                blood
stinging (un)holy water.

They were victims of time.

I visit their homes now, and
the saints weep for mercy.

Denialangerbargainingdepressionacceptancedenialangerbargainingd
epressionacceptancedenialangerbargainingdepressionacceptanceden
ialangerbargainingdepressionacceptancedenialangerbargainingdepre
ssionacceptancedenialangerbargainingdepressionacceptancedeniala
ngerbargainingdepressionacceptance   blame.

They reserve themselves,
build walls around themselves,
praising the suitcases in their attics.
The saints remain   untouched.

A savior means nothing to the already damned.

Bone Shelter
Nannette Montgomery

Night brings a dream.
A house made of women's bodies.
Knees and elbows, spines, and femurs
frame corners, steps, doors and windows.
I step though a gate of arms,
start climbing up steps made of women's backs
like planks they straddle skulls staggering
up a hillside. Great holes stare
out from where eyes once wept.
Clenched teeth yet hold back the screams.
Fingers dangle from eaves of feet.
Waking I find myself curled like an embryo
hugging my pillow.

Hourglass
Kapriah Latifé

Sometimes I wonder
If her hourglass figure
Ever runs out of sand.

Sometimes I wonder
If the grains feel like
The pooling of ice water
In an empty stomach,
Or if they scratch at contact.
Exfoliation to elaborate aesthetics.

Sometimes I wonder
If her frame is made of plexiglass,
To protect its fragility,
If it's porcelain and she is
Just that disciplined,
Or if she cares whether or not
it shatters at all.

Sometimes I wonder
If she feels the sand
Slowly slipping away.
If she inverts herself
To feel full again.

Sometimes I wonder
If she identifies as
The hourglass
Or as the sand itself.

Worth the Weight
Kaely Danielson

A minute on the lips means a lifetime on the hips   they say

because being attractive to the masses is more important

than a bite-sized morsel of a woman's pleasure

and society's image of how a woman
looks is worth more than how
a woman sees

herself.

On every page
we see all we need
to strangle what's left of

a healthy body-image   imagine

what a world of women could accomplish

if our self-worth wasn't squeezed through the narrow

opening of the hourglass our bodies   should   resemble.

Little Motorcycle

JE

"!!! MOTORCYCLE !!!"
She **ROARS** with all the power her little lungs can manage
On her tiny pink motorcycle and little pink snow boots
     I follow behind her

Speeding down the sidewalk
     At 2 miles per hour
She lets out her battle cry
     It's pure excitement and ferocity

Her warpaint?
Copious amounts of glitter and colorful eye shadow
     Done all by herself
She declared she was *cute* when she was done
Her inspiration?
     David Bowie

She turns too hard and tips her little motorcycle
     She cries
Those little rocks stuck in her palms hurt
     And falling is scary
We brush the gravel off her hands and knees
     I give her a hug
I ask if she wants to be done or get back on her bike
     She corrects me
"*Motorcycle*, mommy, **NOT** bike"
She gets back on her *motorcycle* without hesitation

Letting out her battle cry, "*MOTORCYCLE*"
She speeds off down the sidewalk
     I stroll behind her

She's letting the world know
She's here
She's fierce
She's unafraid
She's everything I never got to be
     And I am so happy for her

bikesexual

Anastasia Bamford

it started simply
i squatted on the sidewalk
and watched my dad
remove the training wheels
with a crescent wrench
he gave me
a few words of advice
ran alongside me
then released his hold
and I was flying free
terror was replaced by
the intoxication of speed

i started having secrets
hiding my scraped knees
waiting until i got
around the corner
to cross the street
and explore the
forbidden territories
of the next block

it took years to find her
on that yellow huffy banana bike
streamers on her handlebars
and cards in her spokes
she was the coolest kid
for miles around
with her torn tshirt
and dirty cutoffs
the way she squinted
into the sun
she said that
she liked my ball cap
and i was lost
suddenly
wordless

now i had
a new secret
i began begging
for a three-speed
something to impress her
when i got one
it was pink

i wanted to die

The Joust
Chance Lasher

The sweat had soaked through her linen shirt and pooled in the edges of her goggles; still, Hexer pumped the bellows until they wheezed like an overburdened ox, smelt the tang of sulfur and the stirring of coal and soot as the flames roared in the furnace of the open air smithy.

She tied her thick black hair up in a bun, cinched it with a nail, but the wretched summer heat was inescapable. Master Macchi had picked a grand time to have the day off and leave her with all the orders. Damned if she wasn't going to start her own forge soon, set her own plans in motion. Then Macchi couldn't take his percentage, or get near her *ideas.*

When she was satisfied, she pulled out the horseshoe, glowing like the evening sun, and bent it over the horn of the anvil. She raised her hammer to give it hell—

A golden spider perched on the anvil. The size of her hand.

"Hello, Hexer," it said in a deep monotone voice. "I Have A Message—"

Hexer yelped. Swung. Her hammer smote the anvil hard where the spider had just been. Damn thing had leaped to the floor, scuttled with crimped legs. She saw its bloody ruby thorax slip under the workbench—creepy thing was fast. Hexer ripped off her goggles and crouched, hammer poised to flatten.

"Hexer," the voice said. "It Is Me, Golem. Do Not Destroy My Body, It's Fragile As It Is."

"Golem?" Hexer squinted. It *did* sound like his voice. "The Golem I know stands at least eight feet tall."

"That Body Was Struck By Lightning And Cast Off A Cliff. I Am Now A Spider."

"What?"

"Listen. Den Riggsbold Needs Your Help."

Hex grunted. With tongs, she scooped the horseshoe from the floor and thrust it back in the fire. Pumped the bellows for good measure. Den Riggsbold, one of the rat bastards who cheated her out of coin. Hex owed many debts, and an especially substantial debt to Cardefallo, a suave mason and a merciless gambler who was a regular at the table, along with the goblin. Never again, she'd tell herself each time she lost another hand. Both of them were cheats.

"Not interested," she said. The shoe was hot again, back on the anvil. "I'm working off my debt honestly. Not through favors." She hammered, bent the shoe into a perfect curve.

"It Is Not Gold He Requires," said Golem. "He Is Trying To Avoid The Dead Man's Sloop."

Hexer raised her hammer, stopped. Every criminal in Isa Augusta would rather chop off their hand and offer it to the Duxan than hang in the gibbets—sloops, as they were lovingly referred to—that dangled over the Isebellian Ocean. And who could blame them? There were countless stories of men going mad as they rocked against the high cliff face, left exposed for weeks in the sun and wind, nothing but the churning sea below them. It was said you'd be lucky if sea winds whipped you numb, 'cause then you wouldn't feel your flesh being stripped from your bones when the falcons came to roost.

Hexer grabbed the forepunch from the bench. "The hell'd he do?"

"He Was Caught Stealing Jewels From Sir Poniard's Manor."

"Doesn't he get enough money from cheating at dice?" She hammered the punch into the shoe. Nail holes, over and over and over.

"He Bet Against Another Master Thief To See Who Could Steal The Most From Poniard's Coffer—But Listen. Den Needs To Win A Joust Against Sir Poniard. Otherwise, He Will Be Hung On The Dead Man's Sloop."

"A goblin? Win a joust?" Hex grinned up to her ears. "I didn't know you had a sense of humor."

"This Is Not Humorous," said Golem. "Den Must Win, And He Needs A Mount."

"On a horse," she said, laughing. "His legs wouldn't even reach the stirrups! And Sir Poniard, the champion of the bout, the showman of Argesus? He'll skewer Den and parade him like a flag." Hex snickered and punched another hole. That'll be one debt taken care of. Then she could focus on Cardefallo.

The golden spider stared blankly at her, the polished surface of its ruby reflecting the flames from the forge. Hex ignored it as she punched her holes, and still it hovered, oblivious to her disinterest. "Den Said You Would Help," Golem said. "I Know You Have A Device That Could Assist Him."

Hexer stiffened. "What are you talking about?"

"The Device You Keep In Your Abode With The Wheels And Gears—"

"How do you know about that? You've been snooping around my place?"

"Yes. On Several Occasions." The spider ticked across the bricks, keeping a distance. "And You've Told Den How This Device Will Reinvent Travel In The City."

"Like hell I did."

"You Had Imbibed Many Mugs Of Ale. He Said You Told The Whole Table."

Hexer scowled. So she'd been known to be a driveller when she was in her cups. That was a fact. She started to remember now, the crooked faces leering over their cards as she shared. Cardefallo laughing. Sure, *Hexy*, make an ass of yourself. How about another round? Boy, did that burn her, more than any heat of any furnace could. "It's not for jousting," she growled. "And I don't sell horses."

"Den Says Horses Are Devilspawn Who Delight In Breaking Bones. He Does Not Want One. He Wants Help. He Would Clear All Your Debts To Both Him And Cardefallo."

Hex set the hammer down, stared hard at the spider. Debts cleared. Den, jousting Sir Poniard. Suicide, no doubt. Poniard was the son of a high ranking Duxan, he loved his public image, all the young maidens swooned after him—of course he'd joust a goblin. Another show to bolster his image. How the nobles would gawk, it would draw a crowd just curious to see a goblin, and especially delight in his destruction. Hundreds of eyes, watching the goblin. If Den was riding her bicycle...

"When is the joust?" she asked.

"Tomorrow At Noon."

She grunted, tossed up her hammer, caught it, tossed it again. "Not a lot of time, huh?" She wasn't going to rely on Den to pay off her debt. She could do that herself if the right nobleman was watching. Someone who knew the worth of ideas, the revolution it meant. Mail, delivered within the city by bike. A new form of relaxation. A faster form of travel. Sell that idea and she could pay off all her debt, have her own forge.

"It'll need adjustments," she said at length. "Height, for one thing. Covers for the wheel spokes, a bit of plate armor..."

The spider skittered closer. "Can You Have The Device Ready By Tomorrow?"

60

Hexer's eyes fell back to the horseshoe on the anvil. The glow had dimmed back to dirty steel. Nail holes still needed punching. We have to keep customers, Macchi said, we make things people *need*. And she hadn't made enough horseshoes today. Shoe, nail, drudgery, stuck in old ways.

"Only if I start now," she said, and tossed the unfinished piece into the bin with a clang. Horseshoes could wait.

Enjoying the antics of Den and Golem? Then rejoice! They shall ride again in the next anthology from the Duluth Failed Poets Society!

Acknowledgements

This work has been a true labor of love, and it could not have been accomplished without the unique talents and unyielding determination of Emma Verstraete.

For their creativity, skill, and chutzpah, we would like to thank the contributors and the rest of the Duluth Failed Poets Society. A special thank you to Campbell David, Katie Clark, and Kelli Nogle for their incredible visual art.

For their tireless efforts to inflict truth and beauty on the masses, we would like to acknowledge the members of the Ministry of Truth: Emma Verstraete, Anastasia Bamford, Campbell David, Evan Tungate, Kaely Danielson, Chance Lasher, Justin Rose, Dana Maijala, and Alexander Buelt. We would also like to thank Swerty and Emma Verstraete for their expertise in formatting.

For providing a space for our group to gather and flourish, we are incredibly grateful to Matt and Erin Glesner of The Loch Café and Games. If you build it, they will come.

For giving us regular opportunities to show off, we would like to thank Dovetail Café & Marketplace as well as Wussow's Concert Café. We are also grateful to Studio Café for allowing us to use their space to lay out this book.

For graciously providing funding for this project, we are forever indebted to Jamie Buelt and En Q Strategies. The check is in the mail.

Murderer's Row

Alexander Buelt, the fearless leader of the Duluth Failed Poets Society, believes there's more than enough magic out there in the moonlight. He is working on being happy and knowing it at the exact same time.

Alyssa Stellar is a teacher of many, learner of much, knower of none. She enjoys reading with her cat, Daphne. On the weekends, you can find her outdoors with her partner and her dog, Edgar.

Anastasia Bamford is a queer non-binary poet from Duluth. They are working on their caffeine addiction and evading the authorities while shoving words out of their head and onto the page.

Aubrey Day: "look mom, I'm in a book!"

Bug is on a journey and keeping it sleazy. She loves her very patient husband, yarn crafts, and cats. Peace, love on planet Earth. >;]

Campbell David (tag: Puffinseye) is a visual artist who specializes in charcoal and digital mediums. With a tendency towards maximalism, their work often features witch ladies and tiger centaurs. They can also, sometimes, draw birds :)

Chance Lasher has always lived in the castle. He writes about Golem and Goblin, two troublemakers in a high action pulp fantasy world. Follow him on YouTube @bigbiggoblin2873.

Corey Roysdon is an aspiring author, currently working on getting all of the stories trapped in his mind out and onto a paper canvas. He loves everyone, and you're next.

Dana W. Maijala is a dabbler, chit-chatter, proud mother of two cats-er.

Emma L. Verstraete is the Failed Poets' fairy godmother locked in an ivory tower. When she's not playing with old & broken things she enjoys writing & using ever-increasing arrays of glitter ink.

Evan Tungate is a better poet than most engineers and a better engineer than most poets. He writes poetry and short fiction about moments. His work has previously appeared in *The Tower*.

JE has lost her muchness and is still working on finding it. As such, she doesn't have a bio to share.

Justin Rose writes fantasy novels and audio dramas set in the world of Rehavan, regularly vending his work at comic cons and book festivals across the Midwest. (Oh, he also dabbles in poetry).

Kaely Danielson is a critic masquerading as a writer. She enjoys providing thoughtful feedback and thoughtless jokes to anyone willing to listen.

Kapriah Latifé is a lover of words and the power they have to take something painful and craft it into something beautiful. May others find peace in the words that have healed her soul.

Katie Clark is a visual artist and poet. They are currently pursuing their BFA at Maine College of Art & Design and the other poets miss them very much

Kelli Nogle is the cat sitting nearby, listening and watching. Once in a while, you may find an art she made under your desk, as a treat. <3

Kristina Braaten-Lee moved to Duluth with her husband when she retired from years of wearing her teacher's and chaplain's hats. They came here for the Good Life by the Sea and to be near family.

Nannette Montgomery is a writer and a poet. Her work has recently been featured in *Freshwater Feral*.

Rune Peddle: Star girl, artist, lover of all things alive. Existence is the art itself.

Scott Neby joined a local poetry group to get his body out of the house more. He writes poetry to get his feelings out of the body more. He is uncertain what he gets out of his feelings.

Trae Kryzer is a game designer, novel writer, and local psychopath writing about psychological horror and the ways emotions can physically affect us.

www.ingramcontent.com/pod-product-compliance
Lightning Source LLC
Jackson TN
JSHW061141110325
80467JS00010B/29